The Puppy
who needed a Princess

With special thanks to Anne Marie Ryan

Illustrations by Nina Jones and Artful Doodlers

ORCHARD BOOKS

First published in Great Britain in 2019 by The Watts Publishing Group

1 3 5 7 9 10 8 6 4 2

Text copyright © Orchard Books, 2019
Illustrations copyright © Orchard Books, 2019

A CIP catalogue record for this book
is available from the British Library.

ISBN 978 1 40836 035 4

Printed and bound in Great Britain by Clays Ltd.
The paper and board used in this book are made from wood from responsible sources.

Orchard Books
An imprint of
Hachette Children's Group
Part of The Watts Publishing Group Limited
Carmelite House
50 Victoria Embankment
London EC4Y 0DZ

An Hachette UK Company
www.hachette.co.uk
www.hachettechildrens.co.uk

The Puppy

ho eeded a Princess

Bella Swift

Contents

Prologue

A little puppy with curly brown and white fur trudged along the pavement, her paws weary after a long day wandering the streets of London. All around her, people hurried towards the underground station, rushing to get home after a long day at work. But the

puppy had no home to go to.

Outside the station, a man was handing out free newspapers.

"Oh my goodness," said a lady in a suit, taking a copy. "Queen Eleanor is retiring!"

A man holding a briefcase grabbed a copy from the stack and opened it. Looking up curiously, the puppy saw a picture of a family on the front page – a man and a lady with two children. The little boy was pulling a cheeky face and waving to the camera, but the older girl was hiding her face behind her hands.

"That means the duke and duchess will be king and queen," said the woman, reading the article eagerly.

"That's right," said the man, nodding. "It says the coronation will be next week."

"A new royal family! How exciting!" said the lady, tucking the newspaper under her arm and hurrying into the underground station.

The puppy stared at the newspapers, wondering if she could make herself a bed from one of them. Jumping up, she grabbed a paper from the stack with her teeth and dragged it over to a shop doorway. Scrunching the paper up with her paws, the puppy made a bed for herself in the corner. She curled up in

a ball, imagining that the damp, smelly
doorway was a palace and the hard
ground underneath her was a soft bed.
Soon the puppy fell fast asleep, dreaming
of having a home of her own one
day . . .

Chapter One

A few days later . . .

The puppy trotted down a busy street
on a bright, sunny morning, her tummy
rumbling. As she passed a café she
jumped up, pressing her front paws and
damp black nose against the window.
Behind the glass stood a tower of pastel-

coloured macaroons, éclairs oozing
cream and cupcakes with swirls of icing.
Her belly rumbled again. She hadn't
found anything to eat for breakfast yet
and the cakes looked so tasty . . .

"Shoo!" cried a waiter wearing a
white apron. He waved a napkin at the
puppy, chasing her away.

The puppy sighed and carried on down the busy street, keeping her eyes peeled for dropped food. Spotting a bin, she lingered around it hopefully. A lady approached it, clutching a half-eaten muffin.

This looks promising ... thought the puppy, her mouth watering. But then—

"Ouch!" she yelped as the lady stepped on her paw.

"Oops!" said the lady, throwing the muffin in the bin. "Sorry! I didn't see you down there."

The puppy limped off, her paw smarting, without so much as a bite of breakfast for her troubles. As she made

her way down the street, she was nearly
trodden on several times. London was
always busy, but she'd never seen it quite
so crowded before. There were people
everywhere, and they all seemed to be
holding flags.

Maybe they've come to see the pretty

decorations, she guessed. Bunting stretched
across the street and flags flapped
proudly against all the big buildings.

She saw a smart-looking poodle
walking with a lady who was holding
several shopping bags. *He'll know what's
going on*, thought the puppy.

"Excuse me?" the puppy asked the poodle politely. "Do you know why it's so busy today?"

The poodle just ignored the puppy, brushing past her with his long nose stuck in the air.

But a little sausage dog had overheard her question and stopped for a chat while his human bought a flag from a souvenir seller.

"It's coronation fever," explained the friendly sausage dog. "The new royal family are moving into the palace today."

Of course! thought the puppy, remembering the picture in the paper.

"Everyone's hoping to catch a glimpse of the new king and queen," said the sausage dog. "That's why they're all heading towards the palace."

"Come along, Pickle," said the sausage dog's person, tugging on the leash. "I don't want you catching fleas from that dirty dog."

Hey! thought the puppy, scratching her ear. *Who says I have fleas?*

"Sorry," said Pickle, looking apologetic. "Gotta go."

Suddenly, the puppy's paws tingled and her nose twitched. *Uh-oh*, she thought. Her paws always tingled when there was danger nearby. She looked around.

Nothing seemed out of the ordinary, but her paws had never been wrong before.

Pickle called out a warning. "Watch out!"

Too late.

A man in a green uniform with a shiny badge had spotted her. "Does this dog belong to anyone?" he asked.

The people around him either shook their heads or ignored him, continuing on their way towards the palace.

The man unclipped the walkie-talkie from his belt and spoke into it. "Officer 919 reporting a dog with no collar. Over and out."

The puppy trembled, looking all

around her for an escape route through the sea of legs. Because she knew exactly who it was – the Dog Warden! She'd heard all about him from other stray dogs. He rounded up dogs without homes and put them in cages!

The Dog Warden stepped towards her, reaching out his gloved hands. "Right! You're coming with me!"

Oh, no I'm not! thought the puppy.

The Dog Warden lunged to grab her, but she was too fast. The puppy shot off, into the crowd.

"Stop that dog!" cried the Dog Warden.

The puppy ran as fast as she could,

dodging past people on the pavement.
The Dog Warden's heavy boots pounded
behind her as he gave chase.

She squeezed past a lady pushing a
buggy, nearly getting her paws run over.
"Hey!" cried the lady. "Mind where
you're going!"

The puppy darted out into the bicycle
lane. A man on a bike swerved to avoid
her and collided into a souvenir stand.
CRASH!

"Whoa!" cried the souvenir seller as
T-shirts, mugs and masks printed with
the duke and duchess's faces flew into the
air. Glancing behind her, the puppy saw
a tea towel land on the Dog Warden's

face – but he pulled it off and kept running.

Spotting a park ahead, she sprinted through the entrance. She ran over the grass, past a playground and some flowerbeds full of pansies. Behind her, the Dog Warden's boots thudded louder and louder. He was catching up!

In the distance, the puppy saw a pond with a few rowing boats floating on it. She ran towards it and—

SPLASH! She jumped into the murky water and began doggy-paddling across. When she reached the other side, she scrambled up on to the bank.

Have I lost him? she thought, panting as

her wet fur dripped on to the ground.

No. Her paws were still tingling. She looked back and there he was.

"Stop that dog!" shouted the Dog Warden at the top of his lungs, running around the pond.

Groaning, the puppy sprinted off again. She raced out of the park, towards a big white building with a flag flying from its top. A crowd of people were gathered outside its tall, gold gates, cheering and waving flags. She squeezed through their legs, forcing her way deeper and deeper into the safety of the crowd.

When she reached the front, the gates

opened. As a long, black limousine drove through them, she shot forwards. Luckily, everyone was so busy watching the limousine that nobody noticed the wet little puppy slip through the gates at the same time . . .

Chapter Two

The puppy scuttled around the side of
the building, which seemed to go on for
ever. When she reached the back, she
found herself in an enormous garden the
size of a park. Her paws had stopped
tingling, so she knew she was safe. *Phew!*
thought the puppy. *That was a close call.*

She wandered over to a fountain with
a statue of a dolphin in the middle of it.
Jumping up on to the side, she lapped
cool, clear water from the fountain.
SLURP! SLURP! SLURP!

All that running hadn't just made her
thirsty – she was tired, too. Yawning, the
puppy looked around for a safe place
to take a nap. Spotting a bush with red
flowers, she wriggled underneath it. The
branches were a bit prickly, but anything
was better than the Dog Warden's cage!
She curled up on the mossy ground and
fell fast asleep.

When she woke up again, a few hours
later, there was something – or rather

SOMEONE – next to her! Startled, she yelped and scrambled to her paws.

"Shh!" whispered a gentle voice. "I'm hiding too." It belonged to a girl with dark curls, freckles and friendly green eyes who was lying on her tummy under the bush. She stroked the puppy's soft, curly fur. "Aw," she said. "You're so cute!"

The puppy eyed the girl warily, but didn't run away. Her paws weren't tingling, so she knew the girl didn't mean her any harm. The girl scratched behind her ears. It felt *soooooo* nice! No one had ever given her more than a quick pat on the head before, and the puppy wished it could go on for ever.

The sound of footsteps came crunching down the gravel path and the girl froze. Through the leaves, the puppy could see a lady in a brown uniform. Her grey hair was in a bun and there was a cross look on her face. "PIPPA!" the lady called, putting her hands on her hips. "Where are you?"

"Don't make a sound!" whispered the girl, who the puppy guessed was called Pippa, putting a finger to her lips.

The puppy stayed perfectly still, not even twitching her tail.

"Come out this instant!" called the lady, peering behind the fountain. She headed towards the rose bush and then stopped, so close that her sensible brown shoes were centimetres from the puppy's nose. She could feel Pippa trembling next to her.

"Hmm. Maybe she's gone back inside . . ." muttered the lady, stomping off towards the big building.

When she had disappeared from view, Pippa crawled out from under the bush. "Phew!" she said, brushing dirt off her dress. "That's got rid of Margaret for a bit."

The puppy followed her out, stretching her hind legs and giving herself a shake all over.

"Margaret's my new nanny,"

explained the girl. "She's really strict and is always telling me off."

The puppy wasn't sure what a nanny was, but she assumed it was something like a Dog Warden.

"I wonder what your name is," said Pippa.

I don't know, thought the puppy. She thought she might be called "Shoo", because that's what people usually said when they saw her.

Pippa crouched down and felt the curly fur around the puppy's neck. "Hmm," she said. "No collar. I'm going to call you Rosie, because I found you under a rose bush. What do you think?"

"I LOVE it," barked the puppy, overjoyed. But of course Pippa couldn't  understand what Rosie was saying, so the puppy licked her face to let her know how happy she was.

"Ew!" giggled Pippa, wiping her cheeks. "Now come on – let's play!"

Rosie and her new friend romped across the grass. First, they played hide and seek, with Rosie sniffing out Pippa from underneath a willow tree and behind a bush shaped like a peacock.

There were so many good hiding places in this garden!

"Catch, Rosie!" Pippa called, picking up a stick and throwing it across the perfectly mown lawn.

WOOF! WOOF! WOOF! Her tail wagging, Rosie dashed off and caught the stick in her mouth, then dropped it neatly at the little girl's feet.

"Clever girl," said Pippa, patting Rosie's head.

They played fetch until, exhausted, they both stretched out in the sunshine. Rosie rolled over on to her back, and Pippa tickled her furry tummy.

"The only good thing about moving

here is the garden," Pippa said. "This used to be my grannie's house, but she's retiring and my dad is taking over her job." She sighed. "I wish we could have stayed in the country. It's scary here."

Rosie licked Pippa's hand sympathetically. The city *was* scary sometimes if you didn't know how to look after yourself.

"I get really nervous when I have to meet new people, or when everyone is looking at me," Pippa continued, "but Mum and Dad say it is our duty. Sometimes I wish I wasn't a—"

"There you are!" shouted an angry voice. Margaret the nanny was charging towards them. "Look at you!" she shouted. "Your dress is covered in grass stains!" Suddenly noticing the puppy, the nanny recoiled in horror. "How did that disgusting creature get in here?"

"Her name is Rosie," said Pippa, scooping the puppy up protectively. "And she's not disgusting – she's adorable."

"Put that beast down at once!" screeched Margaret. "She's probably got rabies! I'm calling the Dog Warden."

No! thought Rosie.

"No!" cried Pippa, holding Rosie tight. "She's my friend. I'm a princess – and I say she can stay!"

Rosie looked at Pippa, her big brown

eyes widening in surprise. Suddenly, everything made sense. The big house wasn't just a big house – it was a palace. And her new friend was no ordinary little girl . . . she was a princess!

Chapter Three

Margaret marched Princess Pippa, still clutching Rosie in her arms, towards the big white building. Now that Rosie thought about it, of course it was the palace – that's why everybody had been gathered outside the gates. But she hadn't recognised her friend from

the newspaper photograph, because the
princess had been hiding her face.

"We'll see what your parents have
to say about this," muttered the nanny.
"The duke and duchess have quite
enough to do without dealing with your
mischief. The coronation is only three
days away!"

"I was just
playing,"
protested
Pippa.

"Pah!"
huffed
Margaret.
"You are

a princess, and should always act in a dignified manner. The eyes of the world will be on you this week."

Pippa sighed and buried her face in Rosie's fur. "I wish I didn't have to go to the coronation," she whispered into Rosie's ear. "I'm so scared."

I'll keep you safe, Rosie promised. Princess Pippa had stopped her nanny from calling the Dog Warden, so it was Rosie's duty to protect her new friend in return.

When they reached the palace, they went through tall doors into the grandest room Rosie had ever seen. Pippa set her down on the floor, and Rosie's paws sank deep into the thick, velvety carpet.

Ooh, this is lovely! thought Rosie. It felt squishy, like she was walking on a cloud!

"No!" cried Margaret. "That horrible creature is getting muddy pawprints all over the floor!"

An older man in a smart suit swept into the room. "Ah, Princess Pippa," he said, his eyes twinkling merrily. "I see you've made a new friend."

"This is Rosie," said Pippa, picking the puppy up and offering one of her paws to the man.

He gave it a shake. "Very pleased to meet you, Miss Rosie. Let me know if I can do anything to make your stay at

the palace more comfortable."

"Winston is the butler," explained
Pippa. "He's worked at the palace for
ever."

Suddenly, Rosie's paws began to tingle.
She wriggled out of Pippa's arms and
looked around wildly, trying to find
the danger. Outside the window, Rosie
spotted a man dressed all in black, his
eyes hidden by dark sunglasses. He

looked *very* suspicious.

WOOF! WOOF! WOOF! Rosie
barked, to warn the others. Growling, she
leaped up at the windowsill and knocked
over a huge urn.

CRASH! It fell to the floor, and
shattered into pieces.

"There's a strange man prowling
outside!" barked Rosie, but when she
looked out of the window again, he had
gone.

"This wild animal does not belong
here," said Margaret. "Just look at the
mess it has made."

"Never mind," said the butler. "I can
take care of that." He bent down and

started sweeping up the broken pieces.

A little boy charged into the room, followed by a big grey dog, and flung himself on to the butler. "Give me a piggyback, Winston," he cried playfully.

"Oof!" said the butler. "I'm getting a bit old for that, Prince Henry."

The big dog bounded over and sniffed at Rosie in a friendly sort of way. "Hallo there," he said. "I don't believe we've had the pleasure."

"I'm, er, Rosie." She still wasn't used to using her new name!

"Otto von Weimaraner," said the dog. "Mater and pater are Hugh and Jemima, from the Sussex branch of the family,

you know.
Where are
you from?"

"Um, from around here," said Rosie.

"Then you must know Candy Spencer and Ludo Warren-Mulberry, yah?" Otto wagged his tail enthusiastically.

"Er, maybe . . . ?" Rosie said uncertainly. She was sure if she said the wrong thing she'd end up back on the street. She knew she'd have to go back eventually, but she wasn't ready for this adventure to be over yet! Besides, she'd promised to look after Pippa – at least until the coronation was over.

"Yah, they're always taking Lady Ramona and the Earl of Badminton for walks in Kensington Gardens," said Otto, nodding. "I'll have to introduce you. They're frightfully nice."

To Rosie's relief, a man and a woman walked into the drawing room before Otto could ask her any more questions. Rosie recognised them instantly from the newspaper photographs – they were Pippa's parents, the duke and duchess!

"Daddy!" cried Prince Henry, throwing himself into his father's arms.

"Your Highnesses," said Margaret, curtseying so deeply her knee grazed the carpet.

The duke, who looked like a grown-up version of his son (only with a lot less hair), chuckled and said, "Have these two been making a nuisance of themselves?"

"The princess has dragged this . . . this . . . repulsive CREATURE into the palace," said Margaret, pointing her finger at Rosie.

Rude! Rosie glanced up at Margaret, but as she did so she noticed something alarming – there was a lion in the room! Its sharp teeth were bared and its huge claws were ready to swipe. No wonder Rosie's paws were tingling!

I have to protect Pippa! thought Rosie. Even though the lion was much bigger than her, she ran across the room and attacked it.

BOINK! Rosie bounced off the lion and fell on the carpet. It was just a statue.

Pippa's mum, who had freckles on her nose like her daughter, laughed. Even though she was wearing an elegant suit, she kneeled down on the floor and offered her hand for Rosie to sniff. Rosie wagged her tail and licked the duchess's hand.

"She's not shy, that's for sure," said the duchess, smiling.

"Please can I keep her, Mummy?" said Princess Pippa. "Rosie's really brave – she's not even afraid of a lion."

"A fake lion," giggled Prince Henry. "Even Otto knows the difference."

Pippa ignored her little brother. "Maybe Rosie can show me how to be courageous too."

"Well . . ." said the duchess.

"You said we could get another dog when we moved to the palace," Pippa said.

"I'm sure a filthy stray isn't what your mother had in mind," sniffed Margaret.

"Ahem!" A man in a suit came into the room, bowed and cleared his throat loudly. "Your Highnesses . . . I'm afraid we really must agree the seating plan for the coronation ceremony."

"And the menu!" added a second staff member, holding a clipboard.

"Can Rosie stay, Mummy?" begged Pippa. "Please?"

Rosie stared up at the duchess hopefully.

"I really don't have time to discuss this right now, darling," said the duchess.

"But I don't think she has anywhere else to go," said Pippa.

"OK – just for tonight," said the duchess. "But tomorrow we'll see if we can track down her owner. It's our

duty to see if she already has a home."
As the staff members whisked Pippa's
parents away, the duchess called over
her shoulder, "Do get Rosie something
to eat. The poor little thing looks half-
starved."

"Hurrah!" said Princess Pippa, giving
Rosie a cuddle. "We can play some
more!"

Yippee! thought Rosie, giving her new
friend's nose a lick. She knew her stay at
the place wouldn't last for ever – but she
intended to enjoy every single moment
while it did!

Chapter Four

Rosie trotted obediently alongside Princess Pippa as they wandered past rooms with sparkling chandeliers and beautiful tapestries on the walls. A silver man, his face covered by a helmet, was guarding the entrance to the dining room with a sword. "Back off!" Rosie growled at the man. She didn't want Princess Pippa to get hurt!

"Silly puppy," giggled Pippa. "That's just a suit of armour!"

The dining room was lined with mirrors, which made it look even bigger than it actually was. Out of the corner of her eye, Rosie glimpsed a scruffy little puppy walking alongside a girl who looked just like Pippa. For a moment, Rosie felt confused, and then she realised it was her reflection in the mirror. *That's me!* she thought, amazed. With Pippa by her side, she looked like the dogs she'd seen proudly walking their humans through the park.

When they got to the end of the dining room, Pippa said, "I know the kitchen's around here somewhere . . ." She scratched her head. "The palace is so massive I still forget my way around sometimes, even though I visited Grannie here loads of times."

Rosie's nose twitched. She'd never been to the palace before, but her nose *never* let her down. She could smell something delicious and took off, barking excitedly. She skittered into an enormous kitchen, slipped on the tiled floor and – *WHUMP!* – crashed into a person in a white hat and apron holding a tray. Freshly baked cheese tarts flew through the air and scattered all over the floor.

MUNCH! CRUNCH! GULP! Rosie gobbled them all down.

"I'm so sorry, Eileen!" gasped Pippa, running into the kitchen. "Mum said I should get Rosie something to eat, but I don't think she meant your cheese tarts."

The cook chuckled. "No problem, Princess Pippa. Rosie looks like she needs feeding up. And I could use some help testing out my recipes for the coronation feast. What do you think?" asked the cook, smiling down at Rosie. "Do the tarts need more seasoning?"

Rosie wagged her tail and burped. They were delicious!

Eileen let Rosie and Pippa taste lots of other dishes – from beef Wellington to Welsh rarebit – all served on fancy china plates. Rosie ate so much her tummy bulged. *So* this *is what it's like to feel full*, she thought contentedly.

"Which do you think I should serve as a starter?" the cook asked Princess Pippa. "The mini cottage pies, or coronation chicken?"

But before Pippa could reply, a plump and grumpy-looking Corgi waddled into the kitchen. "Who. Are. You?" she demanded, glaring at Rosie.

"Hi, Constance," said Pippa, giving the Corgi a pat. "I bet you miss Grannie."

"Such a shame Her Majesty couldn't take Constance with her to the tropics," said Eileen.

"Grannie said the heat wouldn't agree with her," said Pippa. She ruffled the thick fur on the Corgi's back. "But we'll take good care of you. And you can play with Rosie."

"Humph!" grumbled Constance. "I can trace my family back twelve generations. As if I'd associate with a common mutt."

She sniffed Rosie disdainfully.

"Aw," said Pippa. "Constance likes Rosie already!"

"Yes," said Eileen, smiling. "I can see that they are going to be the very best of friends."

Rosie stared at the cook in disbelief. Humans really didn't have a clue...

Eileen placed two bowls of vanilla custard on the floor and, even though her tummy was full, Rosie gobbled it up anyway.

"What a surprise – no manners whatsoever," tutted Constance, lapping her own custard daintily.

"Oh, Rosie! You're covered in custard,"

giggled Princess Pippa. "I'd better give you a bath."

"Good idea," said Constance. "She smells like she's been sleeping in a skip."

How did she guess? wondered Rosie.

Princess Pippa picked Rosie up and carried her upstairs, to a luxurious marble bathroom.

"Time to get clean, Rosie," said Pippa, turning on the solid gold taps.

Obediently, Rosie jumped into the water. *SPLASH!*

Brrrr, it's cold, she thought, shivering.

"No," giggled Pippa, fishing Rosie out of the toilet. "Not in there, silly." She put her into the bathtub. It was so big

Rosie could doggy-paddle from one side
to the other! To her surprise, the water
wasn't cold and murky like the pond in
the park. It was wonderfully warm and
full of foamy bubbles that smelled like
strawberries.

Pippa scrubbed Rosie all over
with a flannel that had a gold crown
embroidered on it, washing off the

 custard and the dirt
that had made Rosie's
fur look more grey
than white. "Oh look!"
exclaimed Pippa,
soaping Rosie's belly.
"You've got a spot on

your tummy shaped like a heart. That's the cutest thing I've ever seen."

Once Pippa had got Rosie clean, she rinsed off the suds.

YOWWW! Soap suds ran down Rosie's face, making her eyes sting. Howling, she scrabbled up the slippery side of the bathtub and clambered out of the water – then bolted from the bathroom.

"Come back, Rosie!" called Pippa, chasing after her.

Rosie bounded down the stairs, leaving a trail of wet pawprints behind her. She ran down a long corridor and then suddenly froze. There he was again

– the mysterious man in black!

WOOF! WOOF! WOOF! she barked.
She wasn't going to let him get away this
time!

The man slipped into a room. Rosie
tried to follow, but a pair of sturdy brown
shoes blocked her way.

"You can't go in there!" said Margaret.
"That's the throne room."

"Let me through," barked Rosie, trying
to skirt around the nanny. But Margaret
shut the door firmly.

"Sorry, Margaret," gasped Pippa,
running up and wrapping Rosie in a
fluffy towel. "I was giving her a bath, but
she escaped." She kissed Rosie on the top

of her wet head. "Naughty girl."

"Humph! It takes one to know one," said Margaret sternly.

Later that evening, Pippa had her own bath and got dressed in a pair of silk pyjamas with her initials monogrammed on them. Then she brought Rosie into an enormous bedroom with a canopy bed covered in a pile of velvet cushions and a soft, satin quilt.

Rosie squeezed under the bed and curled up in a tight ball. It was much comfier than a skip – and it smelled nicer too!

"It's unhygienic to sleep with pets,"

said Margaret disapprovingly as she
came to tuck Pippa in.

Hey! thought Rosie indignantly. *I just
had a bath!*

"Rosie needs to sleep with me," said
Pippa. "Otherwise she'll be scared."

Will I? thought Rosie, looking around.
This amazing bedroom was the least
scary place she'd ever spent the night.

She couldn't believe her luck!

When Margaret had gone, Princess Pippa leaned over the side of the bed. "What are you doing down there, Rosie?" she said. She patted her bed. "Come up here with me."

Rosie didn't need to be asked twice. She leaped up on to the bed. Soft as a marshmallow, it was big enough to fit the whole royal family. *Ahh, this is the life*, Rosie thought contentedly, stretching out next to Pippa.

"Actually, it's me that's scared of sleeping here alone," confided Pippa. "It's so big compared to my old bedroom. And Mum and Dad's bedroom is way down the hall." She snuggled closer to Rosie. "But I feel safe with you, Rosie."

Rosie was used to sleeping with one eye open. There was a strange man lurking around the palace, and she knew she needed to stay alert. *Don't worry,* she promised Pippa as the little princess stroked her fur, *I'll keep you safe.*

Chapter Five

The next morning Rosie woke from the best sleep she'd ever had. She'd dreamed that she'd made friends with a princess and spent the night in a palace. Blinking, she looked around and saw Pippa lying fast asleep next to her, one arm flung over Rosie's back.

It wasn't a dream!

Overjoyed, Rosie licked Princess Pippa's freckled cheeks, waking her up.

"That tickles!" giggled Pippa.

"Rise and shine!" Margaret cried, marching into Pippa's bedroom and setting a breakfast tray down on the bedside table. Then the nanny opened an enormous wardrobe, filled with clothes, and took out a frilly dress.

"Yuck!" said Pippa, wrinkling her nose. "I don't want to wear that. Can't I just wear jeans?"

"Your family are posing for an official coronation portrait today," said Margaret. "Jeans are not suitable attire for such an important occasion."

Munching a piece of toast, Pippa went over to the window and peered out. Rosie jumped up on to the window seat next to her, pressing her nose against the glass. Even though it was raining outside, there were still crowds of people peering

through the palace gates.

"I wish they'd all go home," said Pippa, sighing. "I don't like being watched all the time."

"You'd better get used to it," said Margaret, plumping up the pillows on Pippa's bed. "Everyone is curious about the royal family." She bustled out of the room with the empty tray.

"But we're just normal," said Pippa, feeding Rosie her toast crust. "My dad snores and my mum likes dancing to pop music. OK, my brother is a weirdo – he sometimes pretends to be a dinosaur."

Because it was raining outside, Pippa and Rosie spent the morning making a den out of blankets. Snuggling inside the den together, Pippa said, "I wish I could stay in here for ever. Then I wouldn't have to go to the coronation."

I wish I could stay here for ever, too, thought Rosie. *Then I could always keep you safe.* Her paws tingled and her nose twitched – a sure sign that danger was near. *I'm sure it's that man in sunglasses who is always lurking around . . .*

There was a knock at the door and Pippa poked her head out of the den.

"Your Highness," said the butler. "The vet awaits Rosie in the West Drawing Room."

"Thanks, Winston."

Pippa took Rosie downstairs to a pretty room with yellow wallpaper and a beautiful view of the gardens. A friendly-looking lady in a white coat was waiting for them, holding a black medical bag. The duchess was in there too, along with Otto and Constance (who was looking even grumpier than usual).

"Perfect timing," said the duchess. "Dr Beth has just finished giving Otto and Constance their check-ups."

Otto stretched out on the carpet, looking pleased with himself. "I'm fit as a fiddle," he boasted, "but old greedy guts here" – he nodded to Constance – "needs to go on a diet."

"No more table scraps for you!" the duchess said, patting the Corgi on the head.

"This is all your fault," Constance said, glaring at Rosie.

The vet took a stethoscope out of her medical bag. Rosie backed away nervously.

"Don't worry, Rosie," said Pippa, picking her up. "Dr Beth is just going to give you a check-up."

"Up you get, gorgeous," said the vet, lifting Rosie out of Pippa's arms and popping her on a portable scale. She frowned as she felt along the puppy's sides. "She's very underweight."

Dr Beth shone a light into Rosie's eyes.

"Ooh! Too bright!" yelped Rosie.

Next, the vet placed the stethoscope on Rosie's chest, to listen to her breathing.

"Ooh!" gasped Rosie. "That's cold!"

"Stiff upper lip," called Otto.

Dr Beth peered into Rosie's mouth, examining her teeth. "Hmm . . . looks like she's still a puppy."

"Can you tell what breed is she?" asked the duchess.

The vet shrugged. "A bit of this, and a bit of that. Maybe some terrier mixed in with a bit of spaniel?"

Constance snorted. "We didn't need a

vet to tell us that. It's obvious she has no breeding whatsoever."

"I've always found that mixed breeds make the very best pets," continued the vet. "I have one myself. They don't have the health problems you sometimes get with pedigree dogs."

Ha! thought Rosie, though she didn't dare say it out loud.

The vet ran a hand-held scanner over Rosie's body. When it didn't beep, she said, "No microchip, and she isn't wearing a collar. I'm guessing she's probably a stray."

"But she's house trained, so she obviously had an owner at some point," pointed out Pippa's mum.

The vet sighed. "Sadly, some people get puppies on a whim, then abandon them when they get tired of looking after them."

"So we can keep her?" said Pippa, her green eyes shining hopefully.

"Don't get too attached," the duchess said to Pippa. "She might have an owner. We don't know for sure."

Pippa's face fell.

"I'd like you to make some enquiries about missing dogs," the duchess said to the vet. "If Rosie does have a home, we should try to reunite her with her owner. We can offer a reward for anyone with information about her."

"Of course, Your Highness," said the vet. "Now I'd better give her some flea treatment." She squeezed special medicine on the back of Rosie's neck.

"Good idea," said Constance.

Next, the vet held out a treat in her hand. Without thinking, Rosie gulped it down.

"Yuck!" she said, gagging.

"That's a worming tablet," explained the vet. "To keep her tummy healthy. Now there's just one more thing . . ." She took a syringe out of her medical bag. "I suspect Rosie hasn't been vaccinated, so I'd like to give her an injection, just to be on the safe side."

Rosie took one look at the sharp needle and began to tremble.

"Will it hurt?" asked Princess Pippa, stroking Rosie's head.

"She'll barely feel a thing," Dr Beth assured her.

"She's lying," said Constance smugly. "It's *really* going to hurt."

Be brave for Pippa, Rosie told herself.

She felt a sharp jab as the vet pricked her leg with the needle.

Ouch! Even though it hurt just as badly as the Corgi had said it would, Rosie gritted her teeth and didn't let out a whimper.

"You're so brave, Rosie," said Pippa, her voice full of admiration.

And knowing that the princess was proud of her made Rosie feel better than any medicine ever could!

Chapter Six

By the time the vet had gone, the rain had stopped. "Come on," said Princess Pippa, peering out of the window. "Let's go and play in the garden."

"Why don't you take Constance too," suggested the duchess. "She could do with more exercise."

The Corgi groaned. "I'll take a turn around the garden, but don't expect me to join in your vulgar games."

"Margaret will need to go with you," said the duchess, ringing a bell to summon the nanny.

"Why does she have to come?" moaned Princess Pippa.

"We've been through this before," said the duchess patiently. "Things are different now that we live at the palace. We just want to keep you safe."

"But she's always telling me off," complained Princess Pippa. "She never tells Henry off."

"Because he's younger than you," said

her mum. "And you're going to be queen one day and he's not."

"Well, duh," said Pippa. "He's a boy."

"You know what I mean, darling," said her mum. "As the oldest, you're heir to the throne. That comes with certain duties and responsibilities."

Princess Pippa sighed. "Sometimes I wish I were just an ordinary girl. I'm not brave enough to be a princess."

The duchess smiled and stroked her daughter's hair. "Nobody can change who they are," she told Pippa. "And I'll let you in on a little secret. Sometimes I don't feel brave either, but then I just pretend. Nobody can tell the difference."

"Stay on the path," called Margaret, "the grassy is muddy."

"I knew she'd ruin all our fun," muttered Princess Pippa.

Rosie ran over to the fountain and slurped some water, trying to get the taste of the nasty medicine out of her mouth.

Otto spun around on the grass, chasing his tail. "I'll catch you one of these days," he barked.

"Sadly, the vet may have had a point about inbreeding," sighed Constance.

Suddenly, Rosie's paws tingled and her nose twitched. Looking around, she saw

the man in black again, hiding behind a
tree. He was speaking into a headpiece
and staring right at Princess Pippa!

"Get down!" barked Rosie, leaping
on Pippa to protect her. She pinned the
princess down on the grass.

"What are you doing?" shrieked
Margaret. "You'll ruin your dress!"

"Rosie just wants to play," giggled
Pippa, sitting up.

"No!" barked Rosie.
"The bad guy is
back!"

Just then, Winston
the butler appeared in
the garden. "Princess

Pippa, the photographer has arrived. You are needed in the palace." He offered Pippa his white-gloved hand to help her up, as Margaret brushed grass and dog hair off her clothes.

As they all trooped back inside the palace, questions raced through Rosie's head. Who was the man in black? Why didn't anyone else seem worried about him? He was a baddie – she knew it in her paws! It was no coincidence that they tingled every time he was near . . .

The dogs followed their humans into the palace's portrait gallery. It was a long hall, hung with oil paintings of kings and queens.

The rest of the royal family was already there. The duchess looked beautiful in a blue dress, while the duke wore a smart uniform with a red sash and lots of medals. Prince Henry, wearing a smaller version of his father's uniform, was running around the gallery, pretending to karate-chop invisible bad guys.

You don't need to pretend, thought Rosie. *There really is a bad guy around.*

Otto stopped in front of a portrait of a king with a long, curly white wig, his hand resting on a big dog's head. "Ah, there's my great-great-great-great-grandfather, Rex III," he told Rosie.

"Yes, I can see the resemblance," she said.

"He had a terrible limp," said Otto. "Hunting accident. The king was aiming at a deer, but hit Rex in the leg instead."

"Ouch," said Rosie, wincing in sympathy.

They moved on to another painting. This one showed a plump queen holding a fan, next to a table piled with cakes. An adorable Corgi puppy was curled up on her lap.

"That's my great-great-great-aunt, Beatrice," said Constance. "According to my mother, she got so fat she had to be wheeled around in a pram."

"I guess being greedy runs in the family," Otto whispered to Rosie, who stiffled a giggle.

As they walked past more paintings, Rosie felt like all the kings and queens were looking down their noses at her, as if they knew she hadn't descended from royal pets.

The duke introduced Princess Pippa to a man fiddling with a camera on a tripod. "This is our photographer, Luke," he said.

Luke posed the royal family by an enormous window. The sunlight streaming through made the diamonds on the duchess's tiara sparkle.

"Your Highness, could you please put your hand on Pippa's shoulder," the photographer instructed the duchess. Then he turned to the duke and gestured with his hand. "And could you please move a bit closer to the others?"

As the duke shuffled over, Rosie gasped. She could see the mysterious man in black right outside the window. She needed to warn the royal family!

WOOF! WOOF! WOOF! Barking wildly, she lunged towards the window.

"Aww," said Princess Pippa, picking Rosie up. "Rosie wants to be in the picture too."

"No, that's not it!" barked Rosie,

wriggling to get free. "The bad guy is outside!" But when she looked again, the man in black had once again melted into the background.

"If Rosie's in the picture, Otto should be in it too," said Prince Henry. He whistled and Otto bounded over to his side. "He's part of the family."

Rosie noticed Constance looking on sadly. She could tell that she felt left out. Rosie whimpered softly and strained her head towards the Corgi.

"Oh no!" exclaimed Pippa. "We can't forget Constance."

The duchess went over and picked up the older dog. "Of course we can't – she's

been here longer than any of us."

"That's lovely," said the photographer. *SNAP! SNAP! SNAP!* He took photos as the royal family laughed and stroked the dogs.

And even though she knew she wasn't really part of the royal family, Rosie had fun pretending that she was.

Chapter Seven

The next morning, Rosie and Pippa
went down to breakfast in the dining
room. The table was piled with sausages,
eggs and bacon, making Rosie's tummy
rumble. But nobody was eating. The
duke and duchess were deep in discussion
with the palace staff.

"What's going on?" asked Pippa, filling a dish with sausage slices and slipping it to Rosie under the table.

Yum, thought Rosie, gobbling it up. She would miss the delicious food at the palace when she was back on the streets – but not as much as she'd miss Pippa.

Better make the most of it while you can, she told herself, as Pippa added some buttery scrambled egg to Rosie's dish.

The butler brought Pippa a newspaper on a silver tray. "You're front page news," said Winston.

Princess Pippa lifted the newspaper off the tray and sat down on the floor. "Look, Rosie – it's us."

Pippa held the front page up so Rosie could see it. A big photograph showed the royal family laughing and smiling. Prince Henry had his arms around Otto's neck, the duchess was bending to stroke Constance, and Pippa was holding Rosie – who was licking her cheek.

"But Your Highnesses," protested a lady with the clipboard, "this isn't the photograph we approved. We agreed on a formal pose, without the animals."

"We changed our minds at the last minute," said the duke. "We wanted to show the world that we're not just heads of state – we're a family."

"But you're not just any family," said a man in a suit. "You're the royal family. There are certain traditions to maintain."

"Yes," said the duchess, a steely note in her voice. "And we will be making new traditions of our own."

Winston cleared his throat. "Er, Your Highnesses, there have been several enquiries about the puppy, following the newspaper reports. After the reward you offered for information, several people have come forward claiming to be Rosie's owner. They are waiting in the entrance hall."

"What?" gasped Pippa.

Huh? thought Rosie. She supposed it was possible that she'd had an owner once, but for as long as she could remember she'd been on her own.

"Well, I guess that's a good thing," said the duchess. "But I'm quite busy this morning preparing for the garden party."

"I forgot about that," Pippa groaned. "Do I have to go?"

"Of course you do," said her mother. "It's your first official engagement."

Pippa sighed deeply.

"We all need to do our duty," said Pippa's father, tousling her hair.

"Remember what I told you," said the duchess. "If you don't feel brave, just pretend until you do."

"Would you like me to conduct the interviews, Ma'am?" asked Winston.

"I'll help!" Pippa offered quickly.

Winston led Pippa and Rosie into the morning room and went off to fetch the first person.

"Don't worry," Pippa assured Rosie. "I won't let anyone take you away unless they really are your owner."

Winston came back with a lady wearing a T-shirt with a picture of the new royal family on it. She ignored Rosie completely and ran over to Princess Pippa, pinching her cheeks.

"Oh, Princess Pippa, you're even cuter in person." The lady took out a phone and was about to snap a selfie with Pippa, when Winston took the phone out of her hand.

"Sorry, no photographs," he said.

"How about an autograph then?" asked the woman, shoving a poster of the royal family in front of the princess.

"Don't you want to say hi to Rosie?"

asked Princess Pippa, puzzled.

"Huh?" said the lady. "Who?"

"Rosie," said Princess Pippa, picking the puppy up.

The lady recoiled, shaking her head. "Oh, er, I made a mistake. Actually, she's not my dog. She just looks a bit like her. But as I'm here anyway, perhaps I could say hello to the duke and duchess . . ."

Winston politely explained that they were busy, then escorted the royal fan out.

The next person was a man in a smart suit with slicked back hair. "Hiya," he said, handing Winston his business card. "Alec Grant, the best talent agent in the entertainment business. I'm here to offer Rosie representation."

"Representation?" echoed Pippa, confused.

"There's a lot of media interest in this little mutt's story," said Alec. "I can make her millions, get her on all the chat shows—"

"She's a dog," said Princess Pippa. "She doesn't know how to talk."

"Speak for yourself," said Rosie. Of course to the humans it only sounded like, "*WOOF*".

"No, thank you," said Winston, steering the agent out.

The final person they met was a little

boy and his mother. As soon as they entered the room, the boy ran to Rosie and picked her up, squeezing her much too tightly. She could barely breathe.

"Oh, Polly," the boy said. "I've missed you so much."

Polly? thought Rosie, wriggling to get free. *Who's that?*

"We're so grateful to you for finding dear little Molly for us," said the lady.

The boy pretended to cough. "Polly!"

"Oh, er, yes," said the lady. "We thought we'd lost *Polly* for ever. She slipped out of her collar when we were walking near the palace."

Rosie finally broke free from the boy's

clutches and ran to hide behind a chair, her paws tingling in warning.

"Now, I heard there was a reward for finding her owner . . ." said the lady.

Before Winston could reply, Princess Pippa asked, "Does your dog have any distinctive markings?"

"Er," said the lady, her eyes darting around the room nervously. "I can't think of any . . ."

"These aren't Rosie's owners," Princess Pippa told Winston.

"Of course we are," said the lady. She rummaged in her handbag and pulled out a collar. "We can prove it," she said, nudging the boy.

"Here, Molly," said the boy, slapping his thighs impatiently. "I mean, Polly."

Rosie retreated further behind the chair.

"Get over here, you bad doggie," said the boy, grabbing her tail and pulling.

Grrrrr, growled Rosie, her paws tingling more than ever.

"Rosie has a heart-shaped mark on her tummy," said Pippa. "If she really was your dog, you'd know that."

The lady protested, but Winston escorted them out of the room. As they left, the boy burst into tears and wailed, "But you said you'd buy me a new bike if we tricked them."

"That's everyone," said Winston when he came back. "I'm afraid there are some rather dishonest people about."

Rosie's nose twitched in agreement. Her paws were *still* tingling after that close call.

Princess Pippa grinned. "I guess you'll just have to stay, Rosie. Hope you don't mind."

Rosie didn't mind at all! She couldn't think of anything better than staying at the palace with Princess Pippa a bit longer!

Chapter Eight

Margaret came to find Pippa. "There you are!" she said crossly, putting a tiara on Pippa's head. "The garden party guests will be arriving soon. You need to get ready."

"I'm nervous," said Pippa. "I don't want to go unless Rosie can come too

– she makes me feel brave."

"Out of the question," said Margaret. She carried Rosie to Princess Pippa's bedroom and shut her inside.

Rosie clambered up on the window seat and pressed her nose against the window. Outside, in the palace gardens, a big tent had been set up. The royal family stood on the grass, greeting a long line of smartly dressed guests. Rosie wished she could be down there with them to keep Princess Pippa safe.

Pippa was clinging shyly to her mother's hand, her head down. Rosie could tell her friend was feeling scared around all those strangers. Suddenly,

Pippa let go of her mother's hand and ran off. *Something's wrong*, thought Rosie, worried.

A few minutes later, Pippa burst into the bedroom, her diamond tiara askew. "Guess what?" she said. "Everyone is asking to meet you! The guests all saw the pictures in the newspaper and want to meet our dogs. So Mum and Dad said it was OK for you all to come to the party!"

"At least make her look presentable," said Margaret, hurrying in after Princess Pippa with a brush and a shiny red collar.

"Ow! Ow! Ow!" whimpered Rosie as

Pippa tugged a brush through her curly fur. Then the princess fastened a collar around Rosie's neck.

"There!" said Pippa. "You look very smart."

"Ack!" said Rosie. It felt strange to have something around her neck. She'd never worn a collar before, though she'd seen other dogs wearing them when out walking their humans.

"You'll get used to it," said Princess Pippa, straightening her tiara. "Like I'm getting used to this."

Rosie, Otto and Constance trotted outside with Princess Pippa and joined the rest of the royal family.

"I like her collar," said a guest wearing an enormous ruby necklace.

Aw, thanks, thought Rosie, nuzzling the lady's hand. *I like yours too.*

A man wearing a cravat bowed and introduced himself as the Earl of Badminton. "That's a fine dog you've got there, Princess Pippa."

Pippa beamed at the earl. "She's the best. I really hope I get to keep her." She glanced at her mother hopefully.

"We'll see," said the duchess, smiling back at her daughter.

I hope I can stay, thought Rosie. Now that she was by Pippa's side, the princess seemed less shy. She was no longer clinging to her mum's hand and was chatting to the guests happily.

Once all the guests had met the royal family, refreshments were served. Inside the tent there was a buffet of sandwiches, scones and dainty pastries, arranged on silver cake stands. Winston and other waiters moved from table to table, serving the guests cups of tea.

Rosie's paws tingled. Her nose twitched, but it wasn't from the delicious scents coming from the buffet. Danger was near!

Looking around the tent, Rosie suddenly noticed a shadowy figure in the corner. It was the man in black!

Barking wildly, Rosie ran across the tent, bumping into guests.

"Whoa!" cried a lady as her feathered hat flew across the tent like a bird.

Rosie crashed into a waiter holding a tray of teacups.

SMASH! The teacups fell on the floor, shattering into pieces.

But Rosie didn't stop. She bit the man in black's trousers. He tried to shake her off, but stumbled and fell back into the buffet table. *CRASH!* The table broke under his weight, and sandwiches and cakes sailed through the air. A miniature éclair landed – *SPLAT* – on Margaret's head.

Gotcha!

thought Rosie

triumphantly, her jaws still chomping the man's trousers. He wouldn't get away this time!

Drawn by the commotion, the other two dogs ran into the tent.

"Oh I say, this is a jolly good spread," said Otto, gobbling up a plate of scones.

"This sort of thing never happened at Queen Eleanor's garden parties," sniffed Constance disapprovingly. But that didn't stop her from scoffing an entire tray of coronation chicken sandwiches that had fallen on the ground.

"Rosie!" cried Princess Pippa, running over and helping the man up. "Let go! That's Kevin. He's a protection officer. It's his job to keep us safe."

What? thought Rosie. *I thought that's what I was doing . . .*

"Bad doggie!" scolded Margaret. She picked the éclair off her head and threw it on the ground. Constance promptly gobbled it up.

The duke and duchess hurried over looking cross. "Oh dear," said the duke, looking at the mess. "This is a disaster."

"Not to worry, Your Highness," said Winston. "I'll have this tidied up in a jiffy." The butler clicked his fingers and waiters began cleaning up the spilled food.

"Margaret, please take Rosie back

inside the palace," said the duchess.

"But—" protested Pippa.

The duchess shook her head firmly. "No buts. I'm afraid this kind of behaviour just won't do at a royal garden party."

Constance licked cream from the éclair off her whiskers. "I quite agree."

Otto smiled at Rosie sympathetically. "You're in the doghouse, young lady."

"I was just trying to help," said Rosie sadly, her tail drooping between her legs. She felt so silly. Her instincts had never let her down before. The mysterious man in black wasn't a baddie – so why were her paws still tingling with worry?

"You're coming with me, you bad dog," said Margaret. Wrinkling her nose, she picked Rosie up.

As Margaret marched her out of the tent, Rosie peered over the nanny's shoulder and saw Princess Pippa looking sad.

I'm so sorry, thought Rosie, feeling ashamed. She'd let her friend down when she'd needed her most. And worst of all, there was no way she'd be able to stay at the palace now!

Chapter Nine

The next morning, Rosie's tummy was full of dread. As she and Pippa went downstairs for what would probably be her last meal at the palace, Rosie looked around at the beautiful chandeliers and paintings on the walls, trying to memorise every detail. *Well, it's been amazing while it lasted*, she thought gloomily.

But to her surprise, nobody mentioned Rosie's shameful behaviour at the garden party. They were all too busy preparing for the coronation. Eileen the cook bustled into the dining room, holding a cereal box. "Breakfast is just cornflakes," she said, looking frazzled. "I still have hundreds of canapes to make for the banquet tomorrow."

"That's fine," said the duke absently. He was scribbling on a piece of paper – the coronation speech he'd been working on for days.

Pippa held her tummy and moaned

dramatically. "I feel ill."

The duchess put her hand against the princess's forehead. "Hmm. You don't feel feverish."

"Maybe I shouldn't go to the coronation . . ." said Princess Pippa hopefully.

"Nice try," said the duchess, before heading off for a dress fitting.

After breakfast, Rosie and Pippa went out to the garden to play, but everywhere they turned there was a gardener pruning the shrubbery or weeding the flowerbeds.

Hearing a commotion in the distance, Princess Pippa pushed through

the bushes and peered through the
fence curiously. Outside the palace
grounds, well-wishers had pitched tents,
camping out to get a prime spot for the
coronation procession.

"There are so many people," Pippa
whispered to Rosie.

Suddenly, one of the campers pointed
at the fence and shrieked, "O.M.G! Is
that Princess Pippa?"

"Princess Pippa! Princess Pippa!"
cheered the crowd.

Terrified, Princess Pippa froze. Rosie
tugged at her skirt with her teeth, trying
to pull her away.

Suddenly, Kevin was there. "Come

with me, Princess Pippa," he said, guiding her away.

Princess Pippa burst into tears.

"Don't worry, Your Highness," said the protection officer. "I'm here to keep you safe. No-one can get in here without us guards noticing."

I did, thought Rosie, remembering how she'd sneaked into the palace.

Still frightened, Pippa hid behind the rose bush where she and Rosie had first met. Rosie squeezed in next to her. She could feel the princess's heart racing as she snuggled close to her.

"That was so scary, Rosie," said Princess Pippa, burying her face in

Rosie's fur. "I don't know how I'm going to get through tomorrow."

Rosie licked the salty tears off her friend's cheeks.

Pippa smiled. "Thanks, Rosie," she said, hugging her. "I don't know what I'd do without you."

When they went back to the palace,

a van pulled up, escorted by men in uniform on motorbikes.

Oh no, thought Rosie, panicking. *They've come to take me away.*

But to her relief, the men in uniforms weren't Dog Wardens, they were police officers.

Phew!

A guard took a case out of the back of the van and handed it to Winston. Rosie and Pippa trailed behind the butler as he carried the case into the throne room, where the duke was practising his speech.

"Oh good," said the duke, looking up. "The crown jewels have arrived safely." He opened the case, revealing a magnificent crown made of purple velvet and gold and trimmed with white and black fur. There was also a shiny gold orb, a glittering sceptre and a shiny silver sword.

"They're beautiful!" gasped Princess Pippa.

"They're for the coronation," added her father. He placed the crown on his daughter's head. "You look good. Hey," he joked, "why don't you take my place tomorrow?"

"Are you nervous too, Daddy?" Pippa asked, sounding surprised.

Her father nodded. "I'm terrified of giving speeches. But it's my duty."

"You'll be great, Daddy," said Pippa, giving her father a hug.

"So will you, darling," said the duke, putting the crown back in the case. "We both need to be brave."

"Or just pretend we are," said Pippa.

The butler placed the crown jewels and the silver sword carefully in a safe. He twirled the dial to lock it.

"Now we're all sorted for tomorrow," said the duke, smiling.

But Rosie's paws felt tinglier than ever. Why couldn't she shake the feeling that something bad was going to happen?

That night, curled up on Princess Pippa's bed, Rosie was wide awake. Her paws prickled with worry and her nose twitched nervously. Her ears pricked up – a strange rumbling noise was coming from outside Pippa's bedroom.

Rosie jumped off the bed and went

into the hallway to investigate. Her
fur stood on end as she saw a dark
shape looming in the hallway, its arms
outstretched menacingly.

Bravely, Rosie pounced on the shape.
Aha!

But there was nothing under her paws
but the carpet. The scary-looking figure
was just a shadow from a tree outside, its
branches looking like arms.

Feeling a bit silly, she crept down the
hallway. The rumbling noise got louder
and louder as she approached Prince
Henry's bedroom.

She pushed the door open with her
nose.

ZZZZZ . . . zzzzz . . . zzzzzz . . .

Otto was snoring loudly in a basket by
Prince Henry's bed. His leg twitched in
his sleep.

*He's probably dreaming about chasing
something*, thought Rosie.

As she padded back to Pippa's
bedroom, Rosie's nose twitched. She
could smell something.

An intruder! she thought.

She bounded down the stairs,
following her nose. She burst into the
kitchen and saw a terrifying green-faced
monster standing by the hob!

Rosie growled, her teeth bared.

The monster gasped and spilled warm

milk on the ground. *SPLASH!*

"Oh, my goodness," gasped the monster. "You scared me half to death, you silly mutt. I guess you couldn't sleep either."

The monster was just Margaret!

Rosie lapped up milk from the kitchen floor, as Margaret, who had green skin cream all over her face, went back to bed holding a mug of warm milk.

You're just being paranoid, Rosie told herself. But she still felt nervous. She couldn't ignore the tingling in her paws.

Rosie decided to give the palace one final check before going back to bed. As she passed the throne room, a movement

caught her eye. A figure in black was
kneeling by the safe, twirling the dial.

A burglar!

WOOF! Rosie let out a sharp bark of
warning.

Startled, the man turned around. "Shh!
Rosie," he said, putting a finger to his
lips, "I'm your friend."

It was just Winston.

Oh dear, thought Rosie, embarrassed.
She'd messed up again.
Everyone in the palace
would be so cross if she
woke them up in the
middle of the night before
such an important day.

But as she watched Winston open the safe and slide the crown jewels out, Rosie thought there was something different about the way the butler looked – he seemed bulkier than usual.

He's probably getting the jewels ready for the coronation, Rosie thought, cocking her her head to the side and watching curiously.

Winston put the jewels in a bag, then he took the long silver sword out of the safe. It gleamed in the moonlight as the butler ran his finger along the sharp blade. Then standing, he tossed the bag over his shoulder.

Rosie's nose twitched and her paws

tingled so badly she couldn't keep still. There was danger at the palace – and it was right in front of her nose. Winston was stealing the crown jewels!

WOOF! barked Rosie, to raise the alarm. *WOOF! WOOF! WOOF!*

Winston tried to escape, but Rosie bit his trouser leg.

The butler waved the sword, but Rosie wasn't scared. She wasn't going to let him get away – not when he had a weapon that could hurt Pippa!

"Come quick!" she barked.

Kevin ran into the room, followed by a team of security guards. "Drop the bag and put your hands up!" he shouted.

Winston dropped the bag and sword to the floor with a loud *THUNK*.

"What's going on?" said the duke, appearing at the door in a dressing gown and slippers. The rest of the royal family shuffled sleepily into the throne room, yawning and rubbing their eyes. Eileen, her hair in curlers, and Margaret – still wearing her green face mask – followed after them. Otto and Constance padded in, too.

"Not again," said Constance, scowling at Rosie. "I should have known this was your doing."

"I can explain, Your Highness," said Winston smoothly. "I took the crown jewels and sword out of the safe to polish them. I want them to look good for the coronation."

"False alarm," said the duke. "We can all go back to bed."

No! thought Rosie desperately. *He's lying!* But how could she prove it?

Thinking fast, Rosie jumped up and tugged on Winston's jacket with her mouth. *CLATTER! CRASH!* Princess Pippa's diamond tiara fell on the floor, followed by a ruby ring, a pearl bracelet and a sapphire necklace. The butler's jacket pockets were bulging with precious jewellery he'd pilfered from the palace!

Kevin snapped handcuffs on the butler. "I'm arresting you for attempted robbery."

As the protection officer led the butler away, Rosie's paws finally stopped tingling. *It was Winston all along*, she suddenly realised. Every time her paws had tingled in warning, the butler had been nearby!

"You're a hero, Rosie," said Pippa, picking her up and giving her a cuddle. "You deserve a medal."

Rosie snuggled close to the sleepy princess. Knowing that Pippa was safe was the only reward she needed.

Chapter Ten

DING DONG! DING DONG! DING DONG! The sound of bells woke Rosie the next morning. Sleepy from her late night, she burrowed closer to Princess Pippa, who was still fast asleep next to her.

"Time to get up," announced

Margaret, tugging the covers off them. "You don't want to be late for the coronation."

Pippa jumped out of bed and ran to the window. As far as the eye could see, well-wishers lined the route of the coronation procession.

The princess gulped. "Look at all the people."

Rosie licked her hand encouragingly.

"I wish I could be brave like you, Rosie," said Pippa. "Nothing scares you."

Yes, it does. The thought of leaving her friend and being back on the streets frightened Rosie a lot. She'd only known Pippa for a few days, but Rosie couldn't imagine life without her now.

When Rosie trotted into the dining room behind Princess Pippa, everyone cheered.

The duchess set a bowl in front of Rosie. "Eileen has added a new dish to the coronation banquet menu – Steak à *la* Rosie. After all, there wouldn't be a coronation today without you."

"Yah, that was a jolly good show last night," said Otto, wagging his tail approvingly.

"Yes," admitted Constance. "I think there must be some pedigree ancestry in you after all."

Rosie licked gravy off her nose.

Constance sighed. "Though your manners still need work."

Rosie knew that being brave had nothing to do with who your parents were: it meant caring about something – or someone – so much that you would do *anything* to keep them safe.

"What's going to happen to Winston?" asked Princess Pippa, munching her toast.

"We've decided not to press charges," said the duchess, "in light of his long service to the royal family."

"But it's definitely time for him to retire," said the duke firmly.

After breakfast, Margaret helped Pippa

get dressed. The princess's outfit for the coronation was a beautiful white dress with a wide pink silk sash around the waist, and dainty satin slippers.

"I feel like a princess," said Pippa as Margaret brushed her curls and placed the diamond tiara on top of her head. Then she giggled. "Oh, wait. I AM a princess."

"You look positively regal," said Margaret. "For once."

Rosie wagged her tail in agreement. Then Margaret surprised her by giving her a pat on the head. "You look lovely too, Rosie."

They went downstairs, where the rest

of the royal family had gathered. In his smart uniform with the silver sword by his side, the duke was pacing up and down nervously, muttering the words of his speech. Prince Henry, in a matching uniform, charged around waving a toy sword.

"I'm sorry you can't come with us,

Rosie," said Princess Pippa, burying her face in Rosie's fur.

"Actually," said the duchess, "we wanted to give you this." She handed Pippa a gift-wrapped box, tied with a bow.

Pippa opened it and took out a tiny tiara. "But I'm already wearing my tiara," she said, confused.

"It's for Rosie," said the duchess, smiling. "As we haven't been able to track down an owner, we'd like her to stay."

"Rosie has gone above and beyond the call of duty," said the duke. "She's shown loyalty and bravery – we couldn't ask for a better companion for our daughter."

"Yay!" squealed Pippa, hugging her parents.

Rosie couldn't believe her ears. It wasn't that long ago that she'd dreamed about having a home of her own and living in a palace – and now all her dreams were coming true!

"Can she come to the coronation too?" Pippa asked.

"Well, seeing as she's part of the family now," said the duchess, putting the tiara on Rosie's head, "I don't see why not."

The royal family – and its newest member – went outside the palace where a gold carriage pulled by four white horses was waiting for them.

"Good morning, Your Highness," neighed the horses, lowering their heads respectfully, making the plumes on their harnesses bob.

"Oh, you can just call me Rosie," said Rosie, leaping up into the carriage and settling down on the velvet seat between Princess Pippa and Prince Henry. Just because she lived in a palace now and had a sparkly tiara, it wouldn't change who she was.

"Here we go," said the duke, as a

footman flicked the reins and the horses began to trot down the drive.

"Good luck, Daddy," said Princess Pippa.

"We'll be fine," said the duke, smiling across the carriage, the case of crown jewels safely by his side. "We've got Rosie with us, after all. She's our good luck charm."

♡

"Long live King James!" cried the crowd, waving flags as the carriage passed. "Long live Queen Alexa!"

The king, wearing the crown with the fur trim, waved to the crowd. His wife beamed, holding a bouquet of flowers.

Rosie had been impeccably behaved
during the ceremony, sitting loyally
by Princess Pippa's side. The duke had
delivered his speech perfectly, his voice
strong and clear, not betraying how
nervous he was feeling.

"Three cheers for Princess Pippa and
Prince Henry!" cried the crowd. "Hip hip
hooray!"

Pippa held Rosie on her lap and
waved her pet's paw to the crowds as
the carriage rolled past the exact place
where the Dog Warden had spotted
Rosie.

If you're out there somewhere, thought
Rosie, scanning the crowd, *thank you*. If it

hadn't been for trying to escape the Dog Warden, she would have never ended up at the palace!

"You know what, Rosie," Princess Pippa whispered into the puppy's ear. "My mum was right. If you just pretend to be brave, nobody can tell the difference. And that makes you feel brave for real."

SLURP! Rosie gave the princess a kiss. She wasn't surprised that the crowds loved her friend – after all, she loved her too!

As the horses trotted down the city streets, past cheering crowds, the palace loomed ahead in the distance.

"Nearly home," Princess Pippa whispered to Rosie.

The palace had soft beds, delicious food and an enormous garden to play in. But that wasn't what made Rosie the luckiest puppy in the world. Whether you lived in a palace or on the street – and Rosie had tried both – it was *who* you lived with that mattered.

And sitting there by Princess Pippa's side, Rosie knew she was home already.

The End

Love stories about animals?
Read on for a sneak peek …

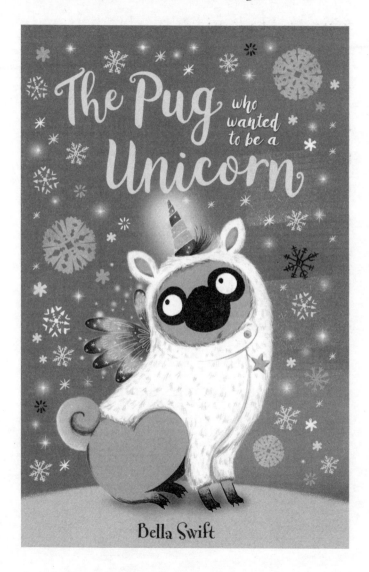

Peggy wriggled her little bottom and snuggled closer to her two brothers and two sisters. The five little pug puppies were curled up against their mother's side, snoozing in a furry heap of paws and curly tails. Sighing dreamily, Peggy nuzzled her squashed black nose against her mum's soft, tan-coloured fur.

Suddenly, her mum stood up, nudging the dozing puppies awake with her nose.

"Hey!" yelped Peggy's brother Pablo. "I was sleeping."

Yawning, the puppies clambered to their feet.

"Today's a very important day for all of you," announced their mum, gazing down at the puppies fondly with big brown eyes. "You're going home."

"Aren't we already home?" asked Peggy, puzzled.

"You're twelve weeks old now," her mum said gently. "So your new owners are coming today. They are taking you to your forever homes."

Read The Pug Who Wanted
to Be a Unicorn
to find out what happens next ...

Have you read all these great animal stories by Bella Swift?

The Pug who wanted to be a Unicorn

Bella Swift

The Llama Bridesmaid

Bella Swift

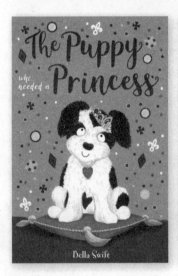

The Puppy who needed a Princess

Bella Swift

The Pug who wanted to be a Reindeer

Bella Swift